My Daddy is a

Air Traffic Controller

Written by Jim McMannamy

Illustrated by Michael Schutz

For Nolan, on his 6th birthday

10/6/2013

My Daddy is an Air Traffic Controller

ISBN 978-0-9899527-0-5

Published by JPM © 2013

Wisconsin, USA

"Okay, class," Said Nolan's teacher, Miss Allie. "Remember that tomorrow you are going to tell your class about your Mommy or Daddy's job."

Nolan was excited. His Daddy is an Air Traffic Controller.

That night, Nolan's Daddy told him (and his brother Indy) everything about air traffic controllers. Nolan had a lot to tell his class, and he was very excited to talk about his Daddy's mysterious job.

The next day in school, right after lunch, it was Nolan's turn to tell his class about his Daddy's job.

"My Daddy is an Air Traffic Controller. He works in a big building called a TRACON."

"Wow, Nolan, that sounds very interesting," said his teacher. "What does he do there?"

"My Daddy works in front of a big radar scope. It's like a TV, except he watches airplanes. He talks on a radio and tells airplanes when to climb up and away from the airport, or when to get ready to land. He tells each airplane which way to turn so they don't get too close to each other while they are flying."

"The TRACON is dark inside, so it's easier to see the airplanes on the radar screen. There are other air traffic controllers that work with Daddy. Every day, the air traffic controllers take turns being in charge. They all work together to help each airplane find the airport."

"Sometimes, when the weather is really bad, like when there are thunderstorms, Daddy has to help the airplanes stay away from danger. He can see the bad weather on the radar screen. Airplanes usually don't mind flying through the rain, but they always stay away from thunderstorms."

Miss Allie was impressed. "Anything else, Nolan?"

"Yes, Miss Allie. Before my Daddy worked in the TRACON, he was an air traffic controller in a control tower. In the control tower, the air traffic controllers tell airplanes when it is safe to take off and land. They also help the airplanes taxi safely. 'Taxi' means to drive an airplane on the ground."

Nolan continued, "After the airplanes take off, he tells them to call the TRACON on the radio."

"My Daddy and Mommy are friends with an air traffic controller who works in a place called a 'center'."

"What is a center?" asked Miss Allie.

"A center is like a TRACON, but it is much bigger. When airplanes fly between far away airports or go way up into the sky, they are watched by air traffic controllers in an 'Air Route Traffic Control Center', or 'center' for short."

"There, the airplanes might be flying much faster and higher than in a TRACON, so they can't fly as close together."

"Some centers have over 300 air traffic controllers working there, but not all at the same time. People are guiding airplanes all day and night, every day of the year, even on Thanksgiving."

"Some air traffic controllers have to get up really early in the morning, and sometimes they even work all night long"

"All of the air traffic controllers in towers, TRACONs, and centers talk to each other on a special telephone. Sometimes in an emergency, like if a passenger on a plane gets really sick, the air traffic controllers call each other to help the airplane get to the airport really quickly. It is one great big team to keep all of the airplanes and passengers safe."

"It's almost time for recess, Nolan. Do you have anything else to say to end your presentation?"

"One more thing. Daddy says that some people see the guys or girls walking next to the airplane with the orange wands and think that they are air traffic controllers. They aren't really air traffic controllers, but they do have an important job to do. It's their job to make sure airplanes don't touch when they park at the airport."

"Okay, Nolan, great job! Thank you for your wonderful presentation to the class. Let's get our coats on and hit the playground!"

Made in the USA
San Bernardino, CA
23 March 2015